Franklin's School Play

For Rachel — P. B.

For Sandi, who was born
to perform — B. C.

Franklin is a trade mark of Kids Can Press Ltd.

Text copyright © 1996 by P.B. Creations Inc.
Illustrations copyright © 1996 by Brenda Clark Illustrator Inc.
Interior illustrations prepared with the assistance of
Shelley Southern.

Kids Can Press Ltd.
29 Birch Avenue
Toronto, Ontario, Canada
M4V 1E2

Printed in Hong Kong by Wing King Tong Company Limited

CDN PA 96 0 9 8 7 6 5

Canadian Cataloguing in Publication Data

Bourgeois, Paulette
    Franklin's school play

ISBN 1-55074-287-6 (bound)   ISBN 1-55074-289-2 (pbk.)

I. Clark, Brenda.   II. Title.

PS8553.O854F73 1996   jC813'.54   C96-930082-4
PZ7.B68Fr 1996

Kids Can Press is a Nelvana company

Franklin's School Play

Written by Paulette Bourgeois
Illustrated by Brenda Clark

Kids Can Press

FRANKLIN could count forwards and backwards. He could remember his phone number, his address and the names of six different shapes. But sometimes Franklin was forgetful. So he worried when Mr. Owl chose him to play one of the lead roles in the class play. What if he forgot his lines?

Every December, Mr. Owl's students put on a show that they made up themselves. This year they would perform A Salute to the Nutcracker.

Franklin had seen the Nutcracker ballet with his parents, and he'd listened to the music at home. He loved the story about a little girl and the toy soldier who comes to life.

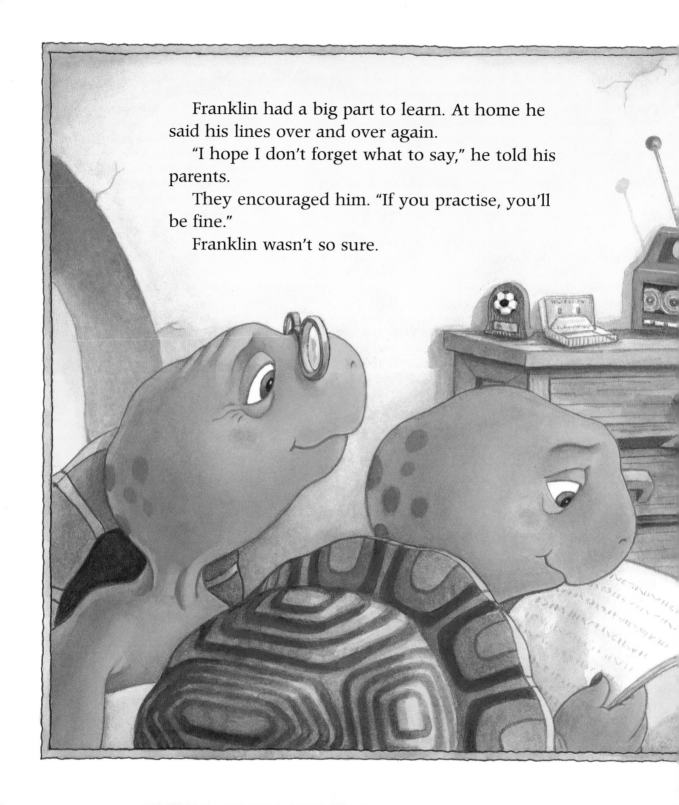

Franklin had a big part to learn. At home he said his lines over and over again.

"I hope I don't forget what to say," he told his parents.

They encouraged him. "If you practise, you'll be fine."

Franklin wasn't so sure.

The week before the show, there was a flurry of activity in the classroom.

Everyone had an important job to do.

Goose studied her lines. Beaver practised her ballet steps. The musicians learned their songs.

"Lovely! Lovely!" said Mr. Owl.

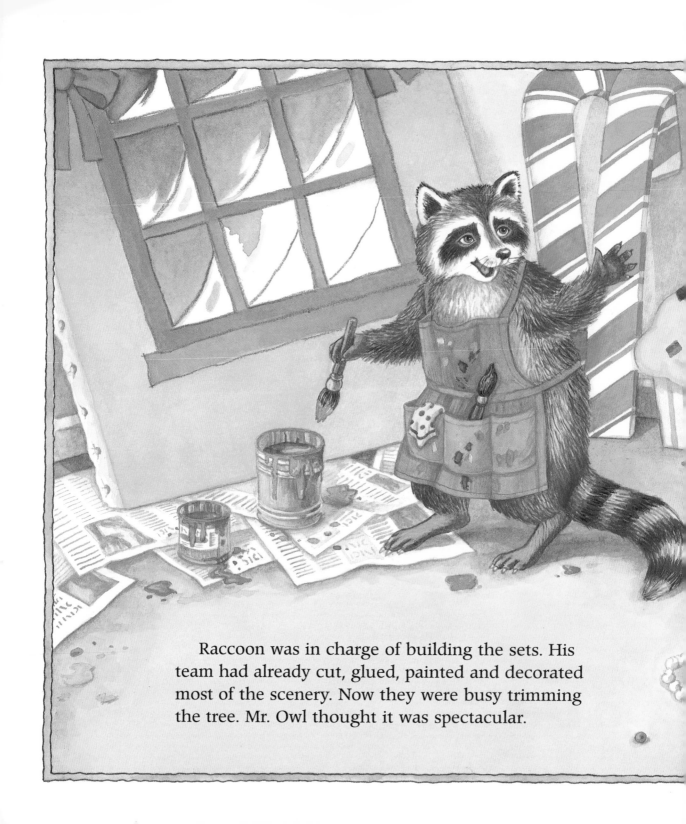

Raccoon was in charge of building the sets. His team had already cut, glued, painted and decorated most of the scenery. Now they were busy trimming the tree. Mr. Owl thought it was spectacular.

Bear was the costume designer. He and his friends created wonderful costumes with bits of this and that.

When Mr. Owl saw what they had made, he clapped and said, "Delightful!"

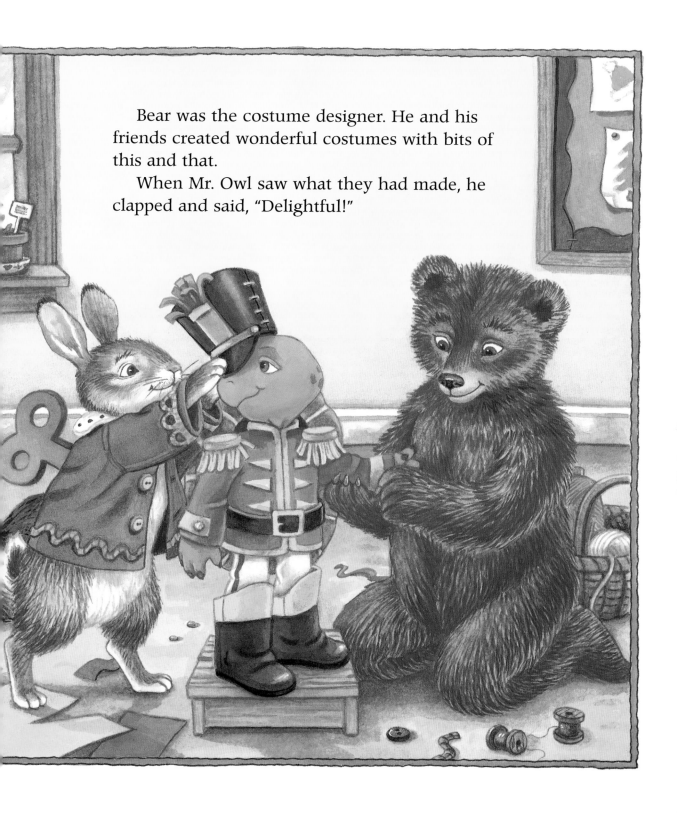

The cast practised speaking loudly and clearly.
Badger was the stage manager so she prompted the
players when they couldn't remember their lines.
"That's great," said Mr. Owl. "But where is Franklin?"
Raccoon pointed to the art supply cupboard.

Franklin peeked out. "I need a quiet place to
learn my lines," he said. "I get to the middle and
then I forget."

"Let's work on them together," suggested Mr. Owl.

By the end of the day, Franklin could say his lines
without missing a word.

"Bravo!" said Mr. Owl.

It was the day before the show. The programs were printed and the seats were set up. For the first time, the students would practise on stage. Mr. Owl directed everyone to their places.

Rabbit thumped his feet in excitement.

"Quiet please," said Mr. Owl. "Curtain time."

Franklin went over the lines in his head.

The curtain opened. Franklin was silent.
Mr. Owl whispered, "It's time to begin."
Franklin tried to talk, but his throat was
tight. Every time he looked at the empty seats,
he was scared.

"Psst," said Badger. "I'll tell you what to say."

But Franklin didn't need a prompter. He
remembered the lines. He just couldn't say
them out loud.

Mr. Owl talked to Franklin alone.

"Maybe you have stage fright," said Mr. Owl. "Try not to think about the audience."

Franklin tried three more times. But each time the curtain opened, Franklin's mouth stayed closed.

He didn't want to give up, but they were running out of time. So Franklin asked Mr. Owl if he could switch places with Badger. She could play the Nutcracker Prince because she knew all the lines.

They started again. Badger couldn't be heard at the back of the room.

Mr. Owl nudged Franklin. "Why don't you help her out."

Franklin stood on stage beside Badger. "Try saying your lines like this."

Franklin spoke in a booming voice. He meant to say just one line. But Franklin got carried away and said a whole speech.

When he was finished, everyone cheered.

"You got over your stage fright!" said Mr. Owl.

"I guess I did," laughed Franklin.

Badger looked relieved.

The next night, when the curtain opened,
Franklin saw his family sitting in the front row.
He took a deep breath.

Franklin's first words were soft and raspy. Keep going, he told himself. And he did. Franklin acted so well that he almost believed he really *was* the Nutcracker Prince.

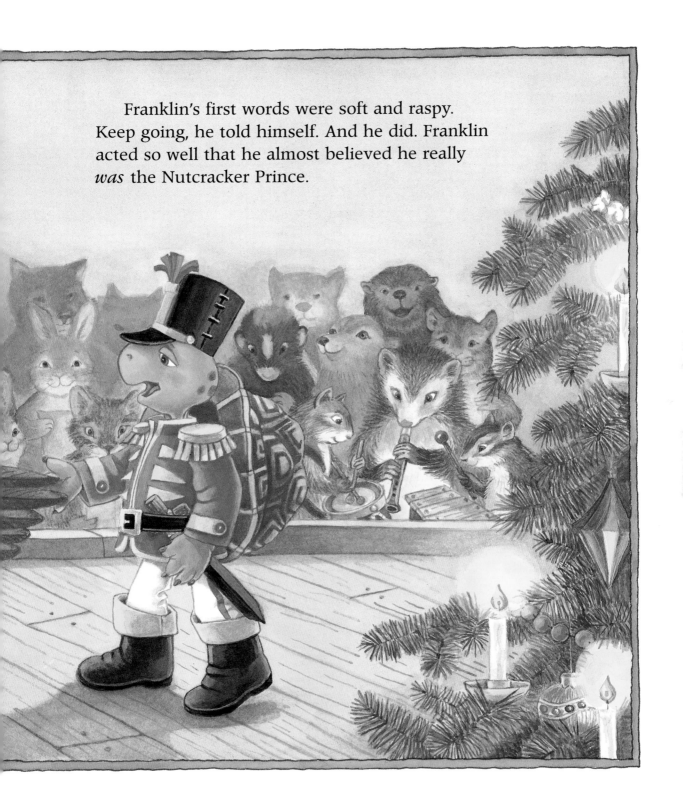

It was a marvellous show. After the finale,
the audience gave the class a standing ovation.
Franklin and his friends bowed four times.

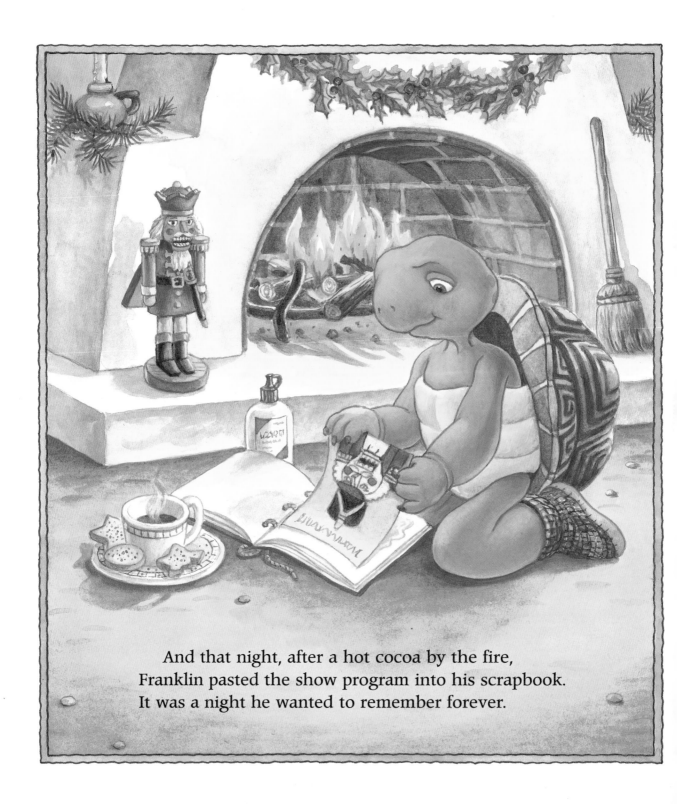

And that night, after a hot cocoa by the fire,
Franklin pasted the show program into his scrapbook.
It was a night he wanted to remember forever.